Stewie BOOM!

and
Princess Penelope

The case of the
Eweey, Gooey, Gross,
and very Stinky Experiment

Written by
Christine Bronstein

Illustrated by
Karen L. Young

To: Caleb, Charlotte, Grace, and Roan,
our blessing makers

Published in 2016 by Nothing But The Truth, LLC
NothingButtheTruth.com

Stewie BOOM! and Princess Penelope: The Case of the Eweey, Gooey, Gross, and Very Stinky Experiment and Nothing But The Truth name and logo are trademarks of Nothing But The Truth Publishing, LLC.
Also available in ebook.
Library of Congress Control Number: 2016932184

Stewie BOOM! and Princess Penelope: The Case of the Eweey, Gooey, Gross, and Very Stinky Experiment
By Christine Bronstein
Illustrations by Karen L. Young
Edited by Summer Laurie
ISBN 978-0-9963074-9-9 (paperback)
ISBN 978-0-9963074-8-2 (hardcover)
ISBN 978-0-9968999-0-1 (ebook)

Printed in the United States of America
Cover design by Karen L. Young
Layout by Jennifer Omner
First Edition

Where does everything go?

WE RECYCLE

- GLASS
- PAPER
- TINS
- PLASTIC BOTTLES
- CANS

COMPOST

- DRIED FLOWERS
- FRUITS/VEGGIES
- LEAVES
- COMPOSTABLE
  PAPERS & PLASTICS

LANDFILL

- FOAM CONTAINERS
- SOME PLASTIC BAGS

My name is Stewie BOOM!
My sister, Princess Penelope, and I like to do experiments. But there are a lot of things about our experiments that our parents do not like.

They do not like when our experiments use up the food we were going to eat for dinner and they really do not like the ones that get eweey, gooey, gross, and stinky.

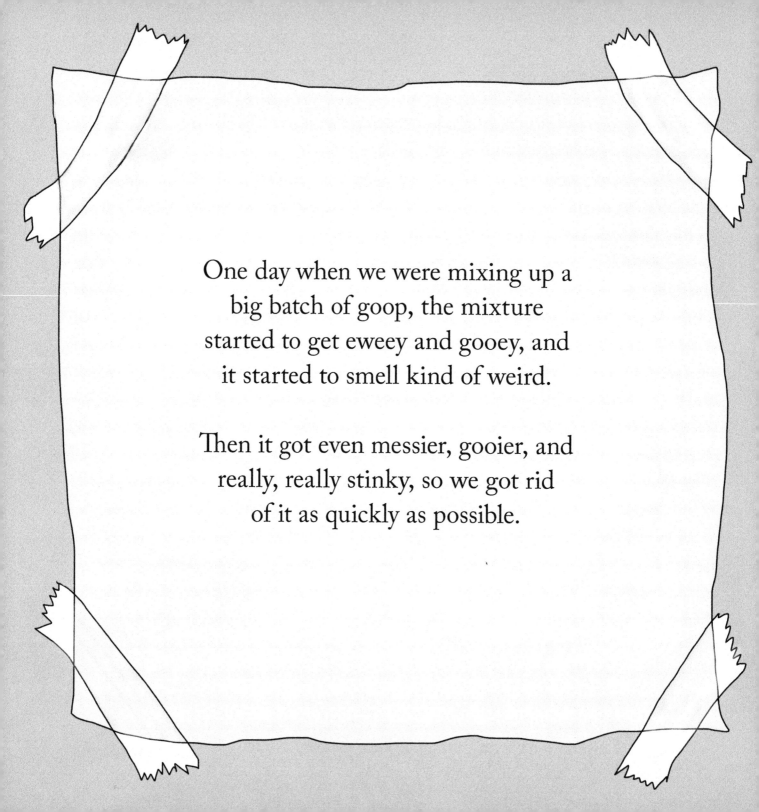

One day when we were mixing up a
big batch of goop, the mixture
started to get eweey and gooey, and
it started to smell kind of weird.

Then it got even messier, gooier, and
really, really stinky, so we got rid
of it as quickly as possible.

We figured everything would be okay.
But, boy were we wrong.

The next morning Daddy asked,
"Why is the yard brown?"

And Mommy asked,
"Why are the dogs green?"

Right then, my brother Zoom
zoomed down for breakfast and asked,
"Stewie, did you take my test tubes
again? I need them for school!"

And then, they all looked at
my sister and me.

"Stewie and Princess Penelope, what did you do?"
Mommy and Daddy asked at the same time.
"We made a potion from stuff around the
house and then when it started to smell weird
we dumped it out the window," I confessed.

"You know you have to ask a grown-up before
you start an experiment," they told me.

"I don't like to be told when
to do experiments!"
I boomed.

But when I looked out at the
brown lawn I felt bad.

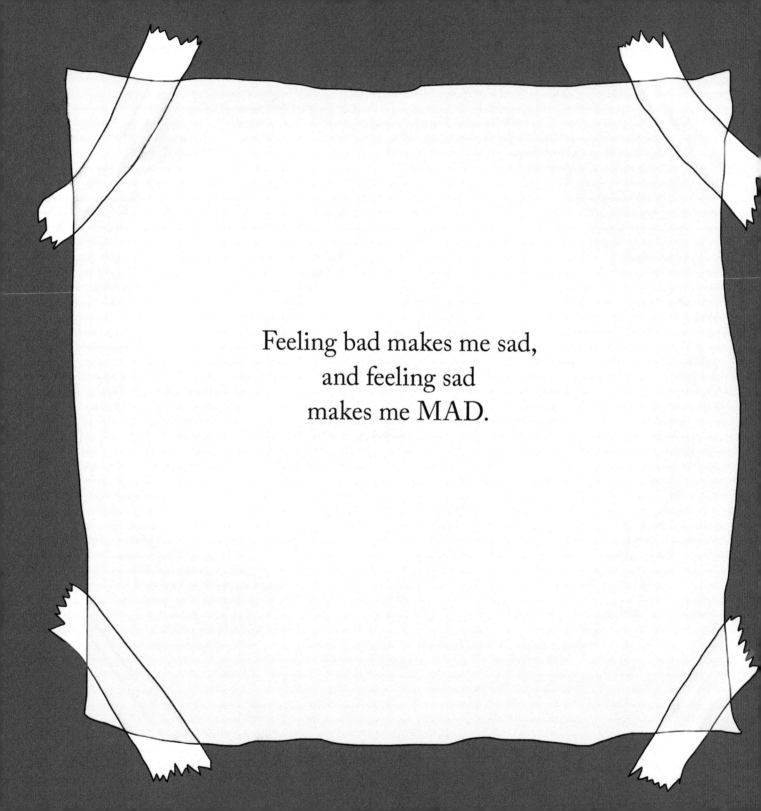

Feeling bad makes me sad,
and feeling sad
makes me MAD.

"It was barely an experiment. We only mixed a few things from the kitchen!" I said as I stomped to the time-out chair where I knew they were about to send me. Princess Penelope pulled up a chair next to me.

"Maybe it wasn't from our experiment! How could a couple of fake cheese chips mixed with a touch of window washing spray and doggie shampoo make the dogs green and lawn brown?" I huffed.

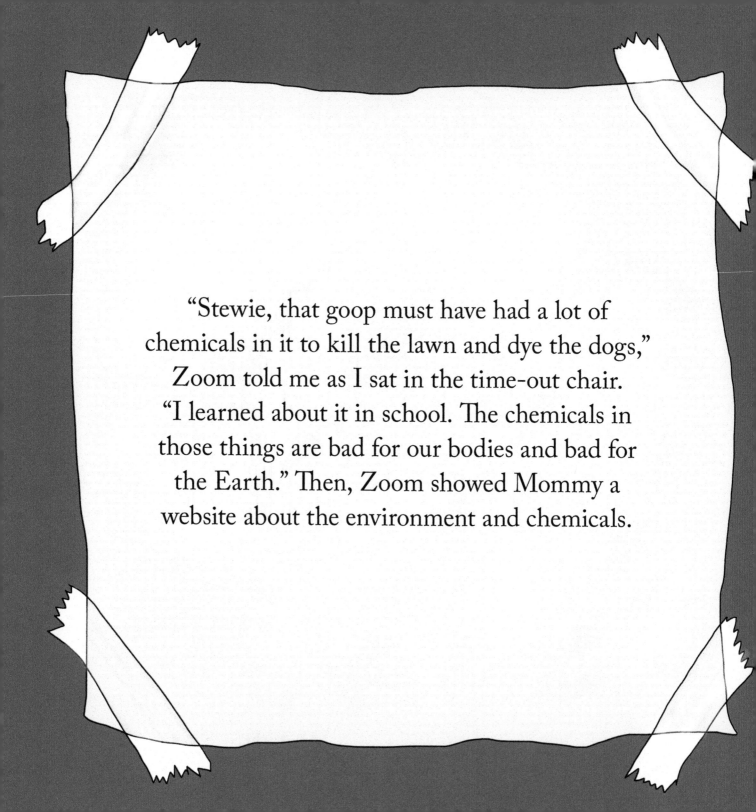

"Stewie, that goop must have had a lot of chemicals in it to kill the lawn and dye the dogs," Zoom told me as I sat in the time-out chair. "I learned about it in school. The chemicals in those things are bad for our bodies and bad for the Earth." Then, Zoom showed Mommy a website about the environment and chemicals.

As Mommy and Daddy tucked me in
to bed that night, I had an idea.

"I know what we can do! We can get rid of
everything yucky in the house!" I boomed.
Mommy and Daddy both had happy faces on
again. "That is a great idea, Stewie," they told me.

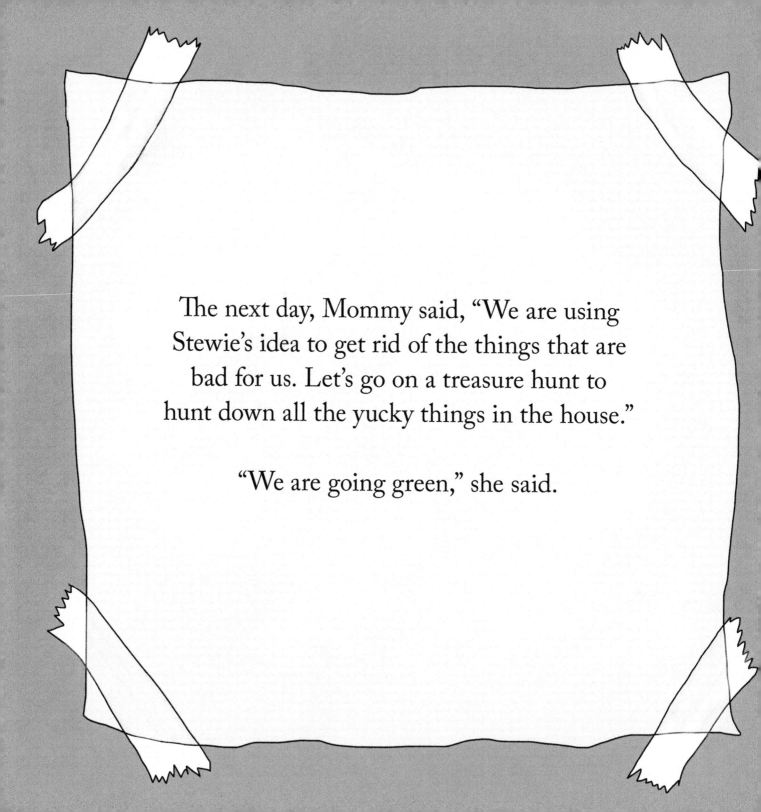

The next day, Mommy said, "We are using Stewie's idea to get rid of the things that are bad for us. Let's go on a treasure hunt to hunt down all the yucky things in the house."

"We are going green," she said.

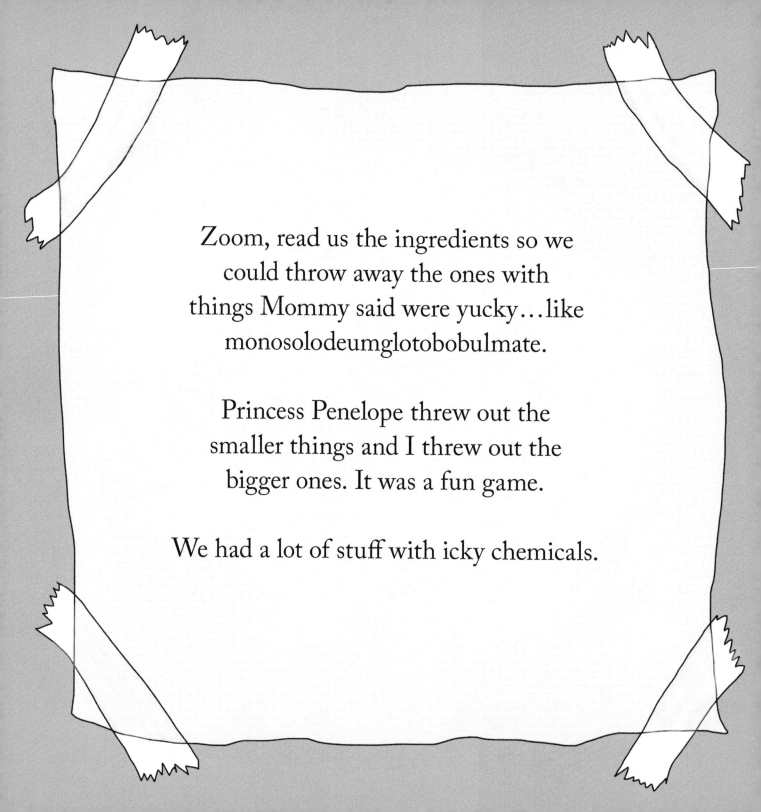

Zoom, read us the ingredients so we could throw away the ones with things Mommy said were yucky…like monosolodeumglotobobulmate.

Princess Penelope threw out the smaller things and I threw out the bigger ones. It was a fun game.

We had a lot of stuff with icky chemicals.

Then, I noticed Mommy was getting rid of my favorite foods and all my favorite experiment materials. It didn't seem so fun anymore.

"This is terrible!" I boomed.

But then Mommy showed me all the new, healthier things Daddy got at the store for us to eat. He even got me some special stuff to experiment with.

"We got organic treats with no chemicals. We even got healthier dog food and cleaning stuff and safe products for our lawn too. All of these things are safe for your body and are also better for our world. It feels good to do our part to make a better world," she told me with a smile.

"Are there other things we can do to make the world healthier?" I asked Mommy and Daddy.

Daddy said, "We can walk to school some days to conserve gas."

My little sister Princess Penelope said, "We can turn off the stuff we aren't using like lights and electronics."

"That's right," Daddy said. "And we can take shorter showers to save water."

I liked that idea. A lot.

So, the next day when it was time to get ready for school, we took fast showers.

We enjoyed our new organic foods. And so did the BOOM! animals!

We recycled our trash and composted
the leftover food from our plates.

And then we
walked to school
with friends.

That night at dinner, Mommy said, "Even though the lawn got wrecked and the dogs turned green, now you two have safe things to mix up, we have safer products to clean with, a place to put our recycling, and healthier food to eat. Because of your experiment we started taking a whole lot better care of our family and the Earth."

She said, "Stewie and Princess Penelope, I think your eweey, gooey, stinky mixture was a blessing in disguise."

That gave me an idea.

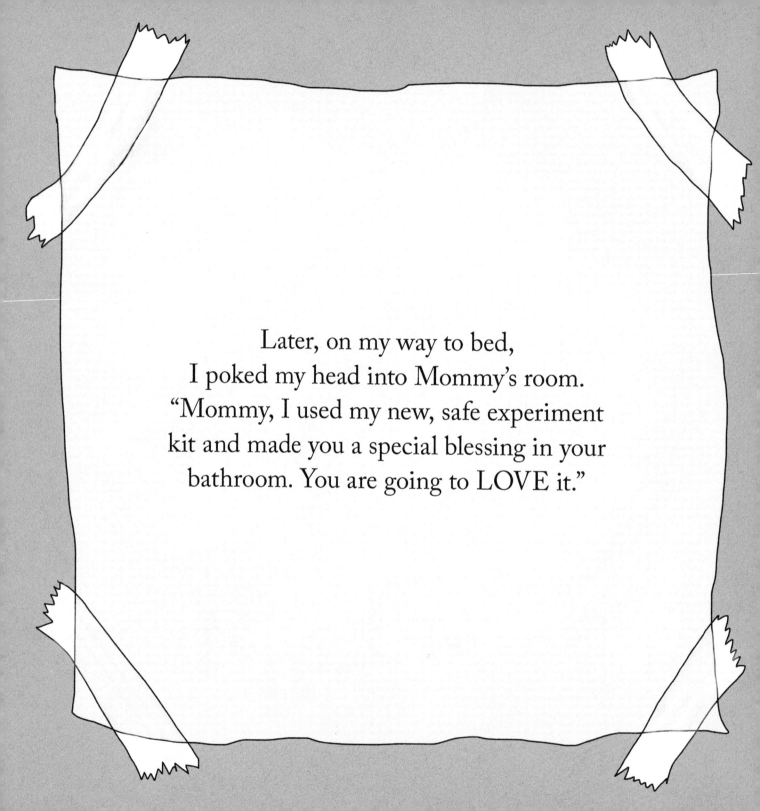

Later, on my way to bed,
I poked my head into Mommy's room.
"Mommy, I used my new, safe experiment
kit and made you a special blessing in your
bathroom. You are going to LOVE it."

The End...

MILK SODA Pizza Daily News JELLY SODA

WE RECYCLE

#1 HELPER

have fun going Green!

Tell us what you recycled & get lots of stars. How many can you get?

7 Stars = 😊 WOW!

BOOKMARK

Protect our Earth

Stewie BOOM!

cut here ↓

www.stewieboom.com

Stewie BOOM!

This bookmark belongs to: _____

Did you get 7 stars?

EARTH HELPER

Awarded to:

_____
(NAME)

Here is your award!

Glossary

compost (lawn): A decayed mixture of plants (such as leaves and grass) that is used to improve the soil in a garden.

compost (kitchen): Many communities have composting programs, in which the trash collectors will remove food scraps and compost them. Composting food scraps is much better for the environment than throwing them away or sending them down the drain.

conserve: To keep (something) from being damaged or destroyed; to use (something) carefully in order to prevent loss or waste.

electricity: A form of energy that is carried through wires and is used to operate machines, lights, etc.

environment: The surrounding conditions or forces (such as soil, climate, and living things) that influence a plant's or animal's characteristics and ability to survive.

experiment: A scientific test where you perform a series of actions and carefully observe their effects.

fertilizer: A substance that is added to soil to make it more fertile and help plants grow.

going green: Making more environmentally friendly decisions such as to "reduce, reuse, and recycle."

organic food: Food grown or raised without the use of synthetic chemicals (e.g., fertilizers, pesticides, hormones), radiation, or genetic manipulation and meeting criteria of the U.S.D.A. Standard National Organic Program.

pesticides: Chemicals used to kill animals or insects that damage plants or crops.

pollution: The action or process of making land, water, air, etc., dirty and not safe or suitable to use.

recycle: To make something new from something that has been used before; to send items (used newspapers, bottles, cans, etc.) to a place where they are made into something new.

repurpose: To alter something so that it can be used for a different purpose.

responsible: Having the duty of dealing with or taking care of something or someone.

toxic: Containing poisonous substances.

waste: To use or expend carelessly, extravagantly, or to no purpose.

A Little Green Goes A Long Way

What does it mean to "Go Green"? When we go green, we make changes and choices that are better for us and for our planet. We appreciate green things like trees and plants because they make oxygen, which we all breathe. Our connection with nature deepens our understanding that we are all connected. When we choose things that are good for our planet, those things are also better for us!

Recycling, composting, repurposing and reusing are all ways to go green. Let's look at a few ways you can start being more green today:

Green Your Kitchen

The benefits of eating food that are fresh and nutritious are well documented. We are what we eat, and our health and wellbeing improves with food that is good for us. Here are some tips on how to green your kitchen:

1. Ditch pesticides by eating food that is home grown and/or organic. Organic farming means that the food is grown without pesticides (chemicals that kill bugs) or herbicides (chemicals that kill weeds). Growing food at home lets you grow food without using pesticides or herbicides. The EWG (Environmental Working Group) suggests always buying the following 12 items from organic farms, since they were shown to absorb the most pesticides:

   - Apples
   - Peaches
   - Nectarines
   - Strawberries
   - Grapes
   - Celery
   - Spinach
   - Sweet Bell Peppers
   - Cucumbers

- Cherry Tomatoes
- Imported Snap Peas
- Potatoes

2. Eat real foods instead of processed foods. Real foods are things like apples, whole grains or milk. Processed foods are things like fake cheese sauce or packaged treats. The more processed a food is, the more likely that some chemical was used to keep it fresh or to give it its color or smell.

3. Use kitchen cleaners that are made with people and planet friendly ingredients. Check out the EWG's website to see how your kitchen cleaners measure up.

4. Avoid bottled water—get yourself a reusable water bottle (make sure it's BPA free if it's made out of plastic) and refill it instead. Then, get a water filter at home! This will help keep your water at home clean and tasting great. Then you can fill up your reusable water bottle at home. It'll taste great and save money!

5. Use the same rules for food as for drinks: buy organic when possible, and avoid overly processed and artificially colored/flavored drinks.

Green Your Bathroom

Did you know that 60% of the stuff we put on our skin ends up in our bodies? Choosing body care that is good for you is important for both your family and the planet. Here are some tips on how to green your bathroom:

1. Check out the EWG's database called Skin Deep. It rates products based on all the ingredients. These ratings (from 1–10) can give you a good idea about which products are most harmful. They even have an app where you can scan the bar code of a product and the EWG rating will pop up! The app makes shopping a lot easier and a lot more relaxing.

2. Avoid these eleven really toxic ingredients in your body care:
- Ethoxylates/PEGs (Including Polysorbates & Sodium Laureth Sulfate)
- Parabens

- Artificial Colors
- Artificial Fragrance
- EDTA
- Phthalates
- DEA/MEA/TEA
- Glycols (Propylene Glycol, Butylene Glycol)
- Triclosan
- Benzalkonium Chloride (including Stearalkonium Chloride)
- Aluminum Salts

3. Bring your old prescription medication to a pharmacy where they can properly dispose of it. Flushing medications down the drain can be dangerous for people and the planet.

4. Turn the water off when you're not using it. When brushing your teeth, turn the water off while brushing.

Greening Your Living Spaces

Many of the room fresheners and cleaners we use in our living rooms and bedrooms are not as clean or fresh as they seem. Look for more natural solutions like essential oil diffusers and green cleaners.

1. Ditch synthetic scents in your air fresheners, perfumes, cleaning supplies and bug repellants by choosing products without synthetic fragrances.

2. Use green cleaners. Even without the synthetic scents, many cleaning agents are bad for people and pets to breathe and they can end up in our water once they're put down the drain. Using 'green' alternatives will be healthier for you and your family.

3. Use an essential oil diffuser instead of a chemical air freshener. The chemicals found in synthetic scents can be really scary. Instead, use some real plant smells to freshen up your home.

Additional resources:

- The Environmental Working Group (EWG) is really a wonderful resource. It can help you learn which products to ditch and which to start using.
- Watch the movie "STINK!"—it's a startling look at what's inside of our everyday products.
- Check out Turning Green, an organization of young people learning how to live healthier.

Susan Griffin-Black is the co-CEO and co-Founder of EO Products. EO stands for essential oils, the essences of plants and flowers that guide every product they make in Marin County, California. EO Products has been making healthy bath and body care for over twenty years under the EO label and the EveryOne label that launched in 2012. Check out EveryOne's Kid's Soap and Baby Collection. They're great for every kid!

Susan is a mom to Marc (aka MarcE Bassy) and Lucy. She has been a student of Zen Buddhism for over twenty years, and you can usually find her in a hot yoga class in the late afternoons.

Fun and Easy Kitchen Experiments

Milk rainbow
Ingredients:
- Plate
- Milk
- Food coloring
- Dish soap
- Cotton swab

Method:
Pour milk onto a dinner plate to cover the surface.
Drop food coloring into the center of the milk.
Dip a cotton swab into dish soap and then touch the tip into the center of the food coloring. Watch the magic happen!

Bubble worms
Ingredients:
- Empty plastic water bottles
- Scissors
- A face cloth
- Elastic bands
- A dish
- Spoon
- ½ cup water
- ½ cup dish soap

Method:
Use scissors to carefully cut the bottom off the water bottle.

Using an elastic band, secure a face cloth over the cut opening of the bottle.

Gently mix the water and dish soap in a dish with a spoon.

Dip the face cloth end of the bottle into the soapy mixture, and blow on the mouth of the bottle to create long, lively bubble worms.

Cornstarch Slime

This is a great little project you can do with kids to show them how certain compounds react to one another, like how the starch solidifies and then liquefies depending on the amount of movement.

For the simplest of all slime recipes, all you need is cornstarch. Just dump some into a bowl, add some water, and start mixing. Keep adding water until it reaches the consistency you want (a good place to start is 2 parts cornstarch to 1 part water). You can also add food coloring to make it look even slimier!

Sparkle Volcano

Ingredients:
- Vase
- Baking soda
- Vinegar
- Food coloring (we used neon red)
- Glitter
- Pan to contain the mess

Method:
1. Place 2–3 Tablespoons baking soda in the bottom of the vase. Put the vase in the pan.
2. Add 6–7 drops of food coloring and 1–2 teaspoons of glitter.
3. Quickly pour in about ½ cup vinegar. Watch for the sparkles!

About the Author

Christine Bronstein is the founder of A Band of Women, a social network and information website for women, a graduate of the Columbia executive MBA program, and author of the award winning *Stewie BOOM! Starts School* and *Stewie BOOM! Boss of the Big Boy Bed*. She is married to Bay Area journalist Phil Bronstein, mother to three wild and wonderful children, three spoiled dogs, and several small creatures.

About the Illustrator

After graduating from Rhode Island School of Design in the mid-nineties, **Karen L. Young** went on to receive her master's degree in Art Psychotherapy. She is the illustrator of the award winning *Stewie BOOM! Starts School* and *Stewie BOOM! Boss of the Big Boy Bed*. Karen is a Vans-wearing, shore-loving, Philly native who now resides in Northern California with her amazing husband, awesome daughter, and crazy Pomeranian.

Visit StewieBoom.com and NothingButTheTruth.com for more information.

CPSIA information can be obtained
at www.ICGtesting.com
Printed in the USA
FSOW03n1927120716
22664FS